Sally Rippin

Lucinda Gifford

BIG DOG LITTLE DOG

Kane Miller
A DIVISION OF EDC PUBLISHING

FOR TYE, OF COURSE.
~ S.R.

FOR MY FAVOURITE SUPPORTERS, DREW,
MAX AND JOE – AND FOR SHEENA,
MY BIG DOG MUSE.
~ L.G.

First American Edition 2022
Kane Miller, A Division of EDC Publishing

Text copyright © Sally Rippin 2021
Illustration copyright © Lucinda Gifford 2021
First published in Australia by Hardie Grant Children's Publishing 2021
Original title: Big Dog Little Dog

For information contact:
Kane Miller, A Division of EDC Publishing
5402 S 122nd E Ave, Tulsa, OK 74146
www.kanemiller.com
www.myubam.com

Library of Congress Control Number: 2021938322

Printed and bound in China
1 2 3 4 5 6 7 8 9 10

ISBN: 978-1-68464-383-7

First there was just Big Dog.

Big Dog had a good life.

Big Dog had everything a dog could ever want.

And his favorite moment of all:

Yes, this was the life.

Just the two of them:
Big Dog and his best friend.
Happy as the day is long.

Even though ...

sometimes ...

the day would be *very* long.

But then ...

one day ...

everything changed.

Little Dog moved in.

Little Dog didn't understand how things worked.

When it came time for **WALKIES**, Little Dog was too slow.

Little Dog didn't
understand **COME!**

He didn't understand **UP!**

And he definitely didn't understand **SIT!**

Now **GET DOWN!** was no fun at all.

Little Dog *had* to go.

Big Dog tried to make his friend see what a nuisance Little Dog was.

Look! Little Dog steals socks!

He pulls food off the table!

He digs up bones!

One day, Big Dog went

TOO
FAR.

That night, no one got *any* sleep at all.

AWROOOOOOOOOOOOOOOOOOOOOOOOOOOOO

AWROOO

Little Dog *refused* to go
to sleep without Big Dog.

The next morning, Big Dog and Little Dog
had **SIT!** together.

They went **OUTSIDE!**
together.

And they played **COME!** *very nicely* all around the garden.

Eventually ...

the house became still and quiet ...

like it always did.

But *this* time ...

the day didn't seem long at all.